D0307855

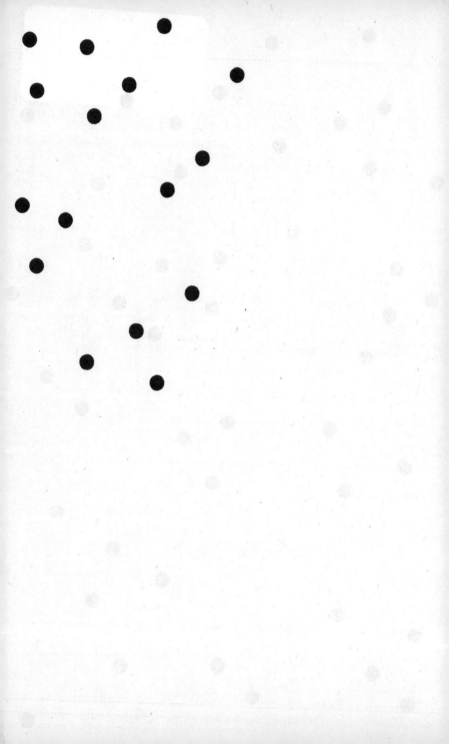

Praise for the Daisy books:

"It must be good. I'm in it!!" *Daisy*

"Don't blame me"
Germius Pavementius

"There'll be no stopping her now
(sigh)" *Daisy's mum*

"What the?!!!!!! Who the???!!!!"
A surprised hippopotamus

More Daisy adventures!

DAISY AND THE TROUBLE WITH LIFE

DAISY AND THE TROUBLE WITH ZOOS

DAISY AND THE TROUBLE WITH GIANTS

DAISY AND THE TROUBLE WITH KITTENS

DAISY AND THE TROUBLE WITH CHRISTMAS

DAISY AND THE TROUBLE WITH MAGGOTS

DAISY AND THE TROUBLE WITH COCONUTS

DAISY AND THE TROUBLE WITH BURGLARS

DAISY AND THE TROUBLE WITH SPORTS DAY

DAISY AND THE TROUBLE WITH PIGGY BANKS

DAISY AND THE TROUBLE WITH VAMPIRES

DAISY AND THE TROUBLE WITH CHOCOLATE

DAISY AND THE TROUBLE WITH SCHOOL TRIPS

DAISY AND THE TROUBLE WITH NATURE

JACK BEECHWHISTLE: ATTACK OF THE GIANT SLUGS

JACK BEECHWHISTLE: RISE OF THE HAIRY HORROR

Kes Gray

DAISY

and the trouble with

LIFE

RED FOX

RED FOX

UK | USA | Canada | Ireland | Australia
India | New Zealand | South Africa

Red Fox is part of the Penguin Random House group of companies
whose addresses can be found at global.penguinrandomhouse.com.

www.penguin.co.uk
www.puffin.co.uk
www.ladybird.co.uk

Penguin
Random House
UK

First published 2007
This edition published 2020

003

Character concept copyright © Kes Gray, 2007
Text copyright © Kes Gray, 2007
Illustration concept copyright © Nick Sharratt, 2007
Interior illustrations copyright © Garry Parsons, 2007
Cover illustrations copyright © Garry Parsons, 2020

The moral rights of the author and illustrator have been asserted

Printed in Great Britain by Clays Ltd, Elcograf S.p.A.

A CIP catalogue record for this book is available from the British Library

ISBN: 978-1-782-95964-9

All correspondence to
Red Fox, Penguin Random House Children's
One Embassy Gardens, New Union Square
5 Nine Elms Lane, London SW8 5DA

MIX
Paper from
responsible sources
FSC® C018179

Penguin Random House is committed to a
sustainable future for our business, our readers
and our planet. This book is made from Forest
Stewardship Council® certified paper.

For Natascha

Chapter 1

The **trouble with life** is it's soooooo oooooooooooo not fair.

My mum says that sometimes life is like that, and that I should take this opportunity to think about things.

It's all right for her. She's not the one having to sit here trying to think about things to think about.

Thinking can be really hard when you're my age. Especially when you're grounded.

Excuse me a minute! . . . I need to go somewhere!!

Chapter 2

The **trouble with being grounded** is it's sooooooooooooo boring.

You absolutely can't go anywhere at all. There's absolutely nothing to do and absolutely no one to play with. Mum says I'm lucky that she's even allowed me downstairs into the lounge after what I've done. She says that most mums would have sent me to my room for about a hundred years after what I've done.

I bet Gabby's mum wouldn't. My best friend Gabby never gets grounded. Even when she drew on her lounge wallpaper with felt-tips, Gabby didn't get grounded.

That's the **trouble with mums**.

You can't swap them for other mums when you need to. Sorry – I need to go somewhere again! . . .

Chapter 3

I don't know why it's called "grounded" anyway. If you ask me, if someone says you're grounded, then it should mean you have to stay on the ground. No hopping and jumping, flying or parachuting. That's what grounded should mean: staying on the ground. Whether it's inside ground or out-side ground, it shouldn't make any difference. As long as you're on the ground you should be OK.

Both my trainers were on the ground in the hallway this morning when Gabby called for me. Gabby is my secret sister. We're in a secret club – in fact it's so secret, only me and her are in it. Every Saturday we take it in turns to be club leader and think of things to do. Last week it was my turn to choose, so we dug a mud trap in my back garden. Then we magicked Tiptoes, the cat from next door, into a lion and tried to get him to fall into our trap. But he wouldn't. He just stayed on Mrs Pike's wall and refused to come down. That's the **trouble with cats**.

They only ever want to do cat things, not lion things.

In the end we had to bang him down with a spade. Gabby hit the wall with the spade handle and I kicked the wall with my trainers. Tiptoes jumped down then all right. He jumped down off the wall on the very first bang. Only not into my garden, into Mrs Pike's. He never comes into our garden any more. In fact I didn't see him on the wall for five days after that.

Gabby says he must have seen us making the mud trap, and it would have been better if we'd magicked him into a hippopotamus. Hippopotamuses love mud.

Gabby's definitely right, so that's what we were going to try today. A better spell and a bigger trap. Except we can't now, because I'm not allowed out to play. Thanks to Mum.

Excuse me a minute. I need to go somewhere again! . . .

Chapter 4

When Gabby called for me this morning, I was dressed and ready and everything. I saw her walking up the path from the lounge window.

She'd brought her own spade to help dig the trap with, a stick for stirring the mud and hopefully some words that rhymed with "hippopotamus". That's the **trouble with writing magic spells**. There are hardly any words that rhyme with "hippopotamus".

I promised my mum I would stay grounded on the ground in the back garden with Gabby. I promised I wouldn't lift my feet up off the grass or anything, apart from when I needed to put my foot on the spade, but she said, "Stop right there . . . Sorry, Gabby. Not today, Gabby. Daisy's grounded. Daisy did something extreeeeemely naughty yesterday and she'll be staying indoors today. I'm sorry to spoil your fun, but it's important that Daisy does some long hard thinking today. She needs to think long and hard about the naughty thing that she did yesterday. And most importantly she needs to learn her lesson."

How poo is that! Uh-oh! I need to go somewhere again . . . !

Chapter 5

The **trouble with long hard thinking**

or even **short hard thinking** is it makes your eyebrows ache.

Especially if you've spent all week trying to think of words that rhyme with "hippopotamus".

Whippo-plop-a-bus, zippy-what-a-fuss, kipper-platypus, drippo-spottiness . . . I've tried absolutely everything. But none of them work.

That's the **trouble with magic spells**: if they don't rhyme properly the magic doesn't work properly either.

Anyway, I've given up thinking about hippopotamuses now. What's the point of having a magic spell that rhymes really well with hippopotamus if you can't use it?

I'm NOT allowed out to play with Gabby today, so we CAN'T dig a bigger mud trap and we CAN'T turn Tiptoes into a hippopotamus. Thanks to MUM, Gabby and me can't do any secret club things AT ALL today. So THAT'S THAT!

My mum says if I keep frowning and the wind changes, my face will stay that way. Well, she should have thought of that before she grounded me. It's totally her fault I can't go out to play with Gabby and it's totally her fault I'm having to frown so much.

I mean, just think. If it had been windy this morning when I opened the front door, my face might have turned into the worst frowning face in the world.

For ever!

And who would have been to blame?

It wouldn't have been me.

It wouldn't have been Gabby.

It would have been Mum! It would have been totally all Mum's fault.

And our front door's.

OOH dear . . . I need to go somewhere again. Back in a minute!

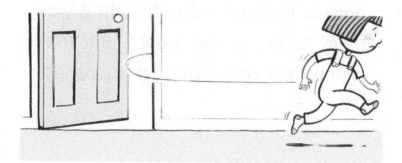

CHAPTER 6

The **trouble with our front door** is
it sticks.

You have to pull it really hard to open
it. I pulled it really hard when Gabby
called for me this morning. I pulled it
so hard I nearly squashed myself
against the wall. Mum thought it was
really funny. So did Gabby. But they
weren't the ones who got squashed.

How would they like to be grounded and squashed at the same time?

The **trouble with being squashed by a door** is it makes you gulp.

And it makes your eyes bulge. Gabby said I looked like a goldfish. Mum said she should take a photo of me and send it to Freddy. Freddy is my goldfish. Was my goldfish. Kind of still is my goldfish. But we had to give him away. We gave him to Mrs Pike to look after. Mrs Pike is the lady next door. She's got a garden pond. That's where Freddy lives now.

I didn't want to give Freddy away. I wanted to keep him and teach him to talk, but the trouble was, he kept jumping out of his bowl.

The **trouble with jumping out of your bowl** when you're a goldfish is you end up on the carpet.

The **trouble with carpets** is they're nowhere near wet enough places for goldfish to live.

Flip knows why Freddy kept jumping out. Mum said it was because I kept feeding him live ants. She reckoned Freddy must have got live ants in his pants and all that wriggling must have made him want to keep jumping out of his bowl.

Trouble is, goldfish don't wear pants.

I think Freddy kept jumping out of his bowl because he thought he was a dolphin. When he was living in the sea before he came to our house, he must have met some dolphins who showed him how to do dolphin tricks.

If I was a goldfish, I'd much rather be a dolphin because dolphins are by far the best fish around. Dolphins know how to stand on their tails without sinking, and they can balance balls on their nose and even jump through hoops. Without ever landing on a carpet.

Freddies can't. That's the **trouble with goldfish who'd rather be dolphins**. They can't do tricks without falling out of their bowl.

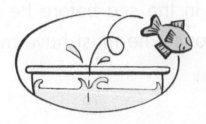

Even if you've got quite a big bowl with weed and gravel in and everything.

The **trouble with weed and gravel and everything** is you have to keep it clean. Otherwise the water in your goldfish bowl goes green.

We came back from holiday once and you could hardly see Freddy. Mum said his water looked like pea soup, which is the worst kind of soup in the world.

Mum said the suitcases would have to wait, and before we'd even unpacked she put Freddy in a saucepan of clean water and then wiped all the green stuff off his bowl with a cloth.

I wanted to have a bath with

Freddy because it would be much more fun for him than a saucepan, but Mum wouldn't let me. Which isn't fair because I was really dirty after our holiday and really really needed a bath with Freddy.

If you have baths with goldfish, you can make hoops with your fingers for them to jump through and teach them tricks that even dolphins don't know!

But Mum said NO. Under NO circumstances am I allowed any alive fish in the bath with me at any time. Not Freddy. Not any goldfish. Not even a very small tadpole. Oo-er . . . Sorry – I just need to go somewhere again! . . .

Chapter 7

The **trouble with tadpoles** is mine never hatched.

The ones at school did. They were in a big jar on the window ledge in Mrs Donovan's class and they hatched all right. And grew legs. And ate bacon.

Mine didn't. The ones in my bucket just stayed like dots. Mum says I shouldn't have put the ham and live ants in until they'd hatched. But I thought if they saw the ham and live ants, they would get hungry and then they would want to hatch quicker. But the ham went mouldy and the ants crawled out. Then the water went smelly. And the dots just stayed like dots. That's the **trouble with frogspawn dots**. Sometimes they don't know what they're meant to do when you put them in a bucket.

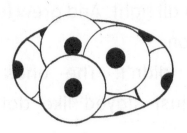

The **trouble with buckets** is the more you fill them, the heavier they get.

When buckets are really heavy, you can hardly carry them at all. Heavy buckets do things they're not meant to do. Which isn't your fault. One day I was helping my mum clean the car and I filled our big red bucket with soapy water. Actually I put the water in first with a hose and then I put some bubble bath in afterwards.

Mum didn't know I was using bubble bath. She thought I was using normal car bath. But I thought the suds would be better if I used bubble bath. And they were. But the **trouble with suds** is they get really sudsy and grow and grow until all you can see is suds, and you can't see how much water is in the bucket.

Which isn't your fault. So when you try to lift the bucket and pour it on the car, the water goes the wrong way and spills all over you. Which isn't your fault either. It's the suds' fault. My mum said it wasn't the suds' fault at all. It was my fault, and if I ever use bubble bath on the car again, she will make me pay for some new bubbles out of my pocket money. Which isn't fair or my fault.

The **trouble with pocket money** is Mum never gives me enough.

I'd like to see Mum buy all the sweets she needs with only the pocket money I get. If you ask me, my pocket money should be at least a hundred— Sorry, got to go again!!!!

Chapter 8

The **trouble with tummy trouble** is you never know when you'll have to run to the loo!

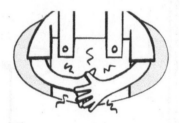

One minute you feel all right and then the next minute your bottom tells you to run up the stairs as fast as you can.

. . .

. . .

It's all my mum's fault I've got tummy trouble.

If she gave me a hundred pounds a week for my pocket money instead of 50p, I wouldn't have run out of money, or got tummy trouble or got grounded. That's the **trouble with having pocket money that isn't enough**: it gets you into trouble. Including tummy trouble.

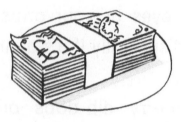

If you ask me, my pocket money should be at least a hundred pounds a week. No – a day. Actually, a minute. Then I'd be able to buy all

the sweets I need without them ever running out.

My mum says that I should suck more and crunch less. Then my sweets would last much longer. It's all right for her. She can control her teeth. I can't. No children can. You have to be at least twenty-fiveish before you can control your teeth. Or your eyes or your arms or your fingers. Especially if it's a strawberry dib-dab.

Strawberry dib-dabs are totally my favourite sweets. The lolly bit tastes all strawberryyyeee and the sherbet feels all lovely and tingly and

fizzy on your tongue. No children can control their teeth when they're eating strawberry dib-dabs. No children called Daisy anyway. If you're eating a strawberry dib-dab and your name is Daisy, then you just have to crunch.

The **trouble with crunching** is, after four or five bites the lolly is always gone.

That's because lollies are always too small.

I tried really hard to suck a sweet once, but in the end my teeth made me crunch. That's the **trouble with not being about twenty-fiveish**.

You just can't control your teeth, however hard you try.

If after about five crunches you haven't got any bits of lolly stuck in your teeth, then the only thing you'll have left is the stick. The **trouble with lolly sticks** is you can't eat them.

If you ask me, you should be able to eat the lolly stick too. If you ask me, all lolly sticks should be made out of more lolly, so that you can eat them all the way down. That's the **trouble with people who make lollies**.

They don't understand how to make good sticks.

They don't know how to put more sherbet in the packet either. Whenever I open my dib-dab packets and look inside, there's always too much air. Even before I've dipped in my lolly, there's loads more room for sherbet. About ten times more at least.

The **trouble with air** is you can't eat it.

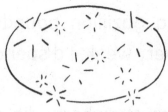

The **trouble with sherbet** is it dissolves too quickly and then turns into air.

And that's without even the slightest bit of crunching.

My mum says I should buy gobstoppers with my pocket money instead of strawberry dib-dabs. But I'd rather buy dib-dabs any day. If I had a gazillion pounds pocket money every week, I'd spend it all on dib-dabs.

Because strawberry dib-dabs are sooooooooooooooooo nice.

Strawberry dib-dabs are tooooooo oooooooooooooooooooooooooo nice.

You can't blame me if they're sooooooooo nice and tooooooooo ooo nice.

It's not my fault if they're lllllllllllll llllllllllllllllllllllllllllllllllllllllllloooooooooo ooooooooooooooooooooooovvvvvvvv vvvvvvvvvvvvvvvvvvvvvvveeeeeeee eeeeeeeeeeeeeeeeeeelllllllllllllllllllllllllll lllllllyyyyyyyyyyyyyyyyyyyyyyyyyyyyyyyyyy yyyyyyyyyyyyyyyyyyyyyyyy.

It's not my fault my pocket money had run out. Or that I had no money at all to buy sweets.

You can't blame me if someone dropped a half-sucked strawberry dib-dab on the pavement outside the shops.

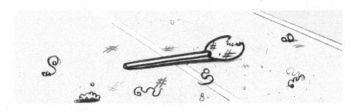

All I did was see it.

. . .

Pick it up off the pavement.

. . .

Put it in my mouth . . .

. . .

And eat it . . .

Excuse me – I need to go to the loo again!

Chapter 9

The **trouble with germs** is they're invisible.

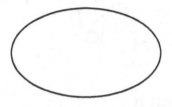

Germius Pavementius

Well, they're either invisible or they're red. Whatever they are, you definitely can't even slightly see them when they're on a half-sucked strawberry dib-dab.

So you can't even slightly blame

me, because invisible is as small as small things get.

In fact it's smaller than that. Invisible is totally teensy.

You'd need a greenfly's eyes to see something that was invisible.

Which absolutely isn't my fault. I mean, sometimes I can't even see the dirty socks on my bedroom floor! And they're LOADS bigger than germs.

I'm telling you, the only thing I could see on that dib-dab was some sherbet. And a bit of dirt which I picked off with my fingers. So how was I to know it had germs on it?

Germius Pavementius
magnified a zillion times

Anyway, I'd licked all the germs off before my mum even grabbed me.

My mum was really really reaaaa aaaaaaaaaaaaaaaaaaaaaaaaaaaaaaa lllyyyyyy cross with me when she came out of the butcher's. In fact her face was nearly redder than the dib-dab.

She said she saw me do what I did through the window of the shop but couldn't run out because she was still paying for the sausages.

That's the **trouble with sausages**.

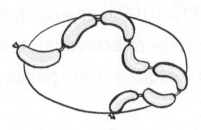

If they didn't take so long to pay for, I wouldn't have had time to put the dib-dab in my mouth.

When Mum grabbed me, she told me to spit whatever it was right out, right now. But she was too late. I was already on my fourth crunch.

"What will people think!" Mum said. "What WERE you thinking of!" she said. Had I gone mad? How could I possibly even think of picking up a dirty disgusting germ-covered sweet off the floor? And EATING IT? EATING ITTTT!!!! Did she not feed me? Had I not had breakfast that very morning? Had I not polished off

a boiled egg and soldiers AND two slices of toast and jam? Or had I had an argument with a witch while she was in the butcher's and been turned into a dustbin on legs?

I wasn't too sure what to say. I thought of asking for some more pocket money, but decided maybe this wasn't the time. So I didn't say anything at all. In any case, it wasn't even a whole dib-dab. It was only a half-sucked one with hardly any sherbet on it. So what was all the fuss about?

The **trouble with not saying anything at all** is it leaves lots of space for other people to say things.

My mum told me off ALL the way home in the car, and then when we got home, she told our neighbour Mrs Pike what I'd done.

Mrs Pike told Tiptoes too and then asked me if I thought Freddy would ever pick up a dirty fish flake from the floor of her pond. Before I could even answer, she told me, "NO HE MOST CERTAINLY WOULD NOT! Not if it was the last fish flake in the world."

Then my nanny and grampy came round to our house to lend Mum their step ladder. When they heard what I'd done, they weren't very pleased with me either. They said that even if they were in the war, when there were no sweets, they still wouldn't have picked a dirty sweet up off the pavement. Which doesn't make sense because if there were no sweets, how could one end up on the floor?

That's the **trouble with really old people**. Sometimes they don't know what they're saying.

Then, just my rotten luck: my Auntie Sue rings up to tell us about her new plasma green telly. Mum tells her about the dib-dab and then hands the phone to me. That's the **trouble with telephones**.

Some people just never stop talking.

Auntie Sue told me all about pavements and then all about germs. She said that once germs get inside your tummy, there's no telling what they can do. Especially if they're pavement germs. Pavement germs can give you diseases and tummy aches and headaches and temperatures. She said germs are like mini monsters. They've got ten heads and fifty eyes and twelve mouths with purple tongues and they love getting inside you so that they can do horrible things to you. Because germs are nasty. Germs are horrible. Germs are out to get you.

No wonder they hide on half-sucked strawberry dib-dabs — Oops, here I go again . . .

Chapter 10

Mum sent me to bed early last night. She said children who eat germy dib-dabs don't deserve to stay up late, even if it is a Friday. Even if there is no school in the morning.

But who cares anyway? I totally wanted to go to bed early yesterday. And double anyway, I had a new comic to read.

The **trouble with comics** is you only get a free gift on the front cover.

I think comics would be much better if you got free gifts on all the pages on the inside too. Then you wouldn't need to look at the comic. You could just play with the free toys.

I got some fly vision glasses in my last comic. When I put them on, they made everything in my bedroom look weird. Every time I looked at one thing it looked like a hundred things. I wore them in the sweet shop last Tuesday and they made even gobstoppers look great.

When I let Gabby try my glasses on in her garden, she said it wasn't fly vision. It was alien vision.

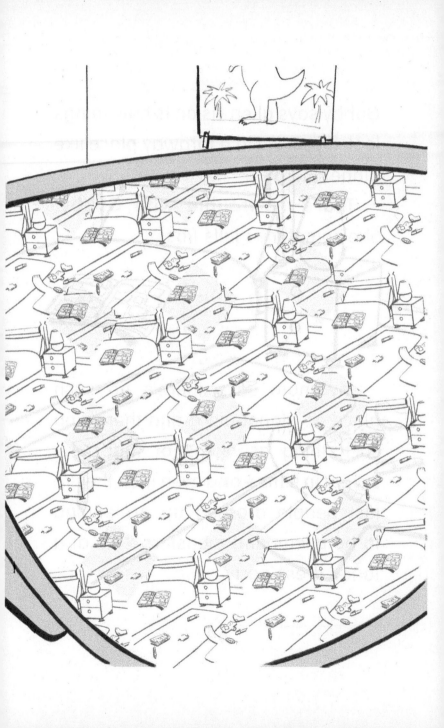

Gabby says alien vision is how things look if you live in a faraway place like planet Blerg.

That's the **trouble with Gabby**. She sometimes tells fibs.

My mum says there's no such place as planet Blerg and there's no such thing as aliens or monsters. Except in films – and even then they're just people dressed up pretending to be aliens and monsters. Like at a fancy-dress party.

That's the **trouble with films**.

They pretend to be real but they're not.

Last Halloween I went to a fancy-dress party and dressed up as a ghost! Ghosts aren't real either. They're just small children with sheets on.

I didn't like being a ghost at first because I couldn't see where I was going. When my mum turned my sheet round, it was much better

because then I could see out of the holes. And I could breathe.

Harry Bayliss who's in my class at school went to the party dressed as a hooley-hooley man with real fake blood and vampire fangs, but Vicky Carrow hit him on the head with her hooley-hooley stick. It wasn't a real hooley-hooley stick – it was a cucumber. Hooley-hooley men aren't real either by the way.

Except they do do real tears.

Harry Bayliss's dad came to collect him and all the monsters and ghosts were told to stop running around like loony ticks.

Vicky Carrow asked me if she could hide her cucumber up my sheet but I told her I needed both hands to eat my sandwiches.

That's the **trouble with party sandwiches**: if you don't take three or four all at once, other children will take all the nice ones.

Billy Laine said he had real bat's blood in his sandwiches. But it wasn't. It was raspberry jam.

So Vicky hit him on the head too.

And then she poked Jenny Pearson in the back for having a witch's nose.

Vicky Carrow's hooley-hooley stick got taken away in the end.

Actually, so did Vicky Carrow.

The **trouble with ghost sheets** is they make you ever so hot.

I was really sweating by the time my mum came to collect me. When I took it off outside by the car, my face went all cold in the fresh air.

Mum jumped when I took my sheet off, and pretended I was more scary without my sheet on. I only smiled a bit. I didn't laugh, because she's done that joke before.

When I got home after the party, I couldn't get to sleep, but when I did, I had a dream about skeletons. Which definitely are real because I saw one in an actual book at school once. Everything in school books has to be real. It's the law.

Anyway, in my dream four skeletons were chasing me!!!! And they were bouncing on big cucumbers like pogo sticks and trying to catch me!

It was really scary but there was nothing I could do, because the **trouble with bad dreams** is you always have to fall over before you can wake up.

But the more I tried to fall over, the more I stayed up. And the closer the skeletons got!

In the end I just closed my eyes and jumped . . .

My mum jumped too when I landed in her bed. She said she was right in the middle of a really nice dream about a handsome prince, who was just about to give her his phone number, when I had woken her up and made him drop his pen.

Which did make me laugh and smile a bit, and forget about the skeletons, because I hadn't heard that joke before. Hold on, I think I need to go to the loo again . . .

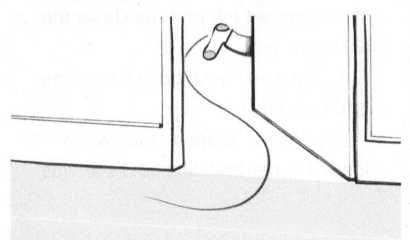

Still Chapter 10

Actually no, I don't. I just thought I did. I'm OK.

In fact I think I'm beginning to feel a bit better!

Last night after I was sent to bed I didn't have any dreams at all. My tummy was too busy gurgling.

The **trouble with gurgles** is they sound really loud when they're your own gurgles. Especially if they're germ gurgles.

Germ gurgles are much more gurglier than normal gurgles.

By the time I'd thrown all my toys at the wall last night, and finished looking at my comic, and pulled all the whiskers off my rabbit (don't worry, he's a toy), my tummy sounded like it was a growling wolf.

When it was evening, Mum came up and pulled my curtains and told me never to pick anything up off the floor again apart from all my toys in the morning. Then she sat on my bed and listened.

She said my tummy sounded like a witch's pot and that trouble was brewing. And she said I only had myself to blame. She said if I hadn't been so naughty and put that dirty sweet in my mouth and eaten it, none of this would have happened.

That's the **trouble with mums**.

In the end, they're always right. And I'm wrong – I do need to go again . . .

Chapter 11

The **trouble with loo rolls** is they always run out when you don't want them to.

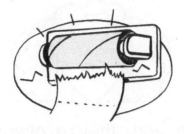

When I ran to the loo the first time last night, I went past Mum's bedroom really really quietly.

That way, she wouldn't know the dib-dab germs had got me.

And that way, in the morning I could pretend there never were any germs on that dib-dab. So then Mum would feel really bad about telling me off in the first place. So would Nanny and Grampy and Auntie Sue and Mrs Pike and Tiptoes!!!!!

Trouble is, when I turned the light on in the bathroom, the loo roll was all gone, apart from the cardboard bit in the middle. And I couldn't use that because . . . well I couldn't. And anyway, I always save that bit for Gabby's hamster. Gabby's hamster loves eating empty loo rolls.

So I had no choice.

"MUM, THERE'S NO LOO ROLL!"
I had to shout.

"WAKE UP! I NEED SOME LOO ROLL,"
I had to shout again.

The **trouble with shouting when someone's asleep** is they don't always hear you.

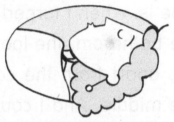

So then you have to shout louder and LOUDER, and kick the side of the bath with your feet too.

"MUM! MUM! THE DIB-DAB GERMS HAVE GOT ME. I'VE GOT TUMMY

TROUBLE!!!! HELP!!!!!!!!!!!" I had to
shout at the top of my voice.

The **trouble with waking my
mum up** is she doesn't really like it.

The **trouble with waking my
mum up when she's in a bad mood**

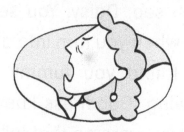

is she REALLY doesn't like it.

I can tell because usually, when there's something wrong with me in the night, my mum pretends to keep her eyes open and rubs my back. But not last night. At least not when she came into the bathroom the first time.

The first time she came to see me, she folded her arms and tapped her toes on the bathroom floor and said, "You see, Daisy. You see what happens when you turn into a human dustbin. I told you tummy trouble was brewing. Goodness knows how many germs were on that lolly."

Luckily we had some more loo

rolls in the bathroom cupboard. Mum bought them yesterday before she went to the butcher's.

Trouble is, there are only twelve loo rolls in a pack.

Oo.

No.

Yes, no, yes.

Not sure . . .

See you in a min . . . !!!!!!!!!!!

Chapter 12

Phew!!

Good news at last! I didn't have to open loo roll number eleven!

In fact, I didn't have to go to the loo at all! Which means I must be getting better!

Which is a good job because the **trouble with brand-new loo rolls** is they can be really tricky to open.

A bit like cheese triangles.

Once, when I was hungry, I tried to make my own picnic, but I couldn't get the cheese out of the triangle at all. Until I squeezed it really really hard with both hands. Then all the cheese squidged out of one end, all over my fingers.

Mum says cheese triangles are really easy to open when you know how.

That's the **trouble with grown-ups**. They know everything.

At least they think they do.

I got most of the cheese out in the end but it didn't look anything like a triangle. Which made me really cross because triangles are my favourite shape. Then circles. Then squares.

I didn't fancy the cheese after that. So in the end I just ate the bread.

The **trouble with bread** is my mum never lets me cut it myself.

She says I'll have an accident

with the big knife and chop all my fingers off. Then I'll have to have a finger sandwich instead of a cheese sandwich, because good fingers shouldn't go to waste.

Anyway, how could I pick up a finger sandwich if all my fingers were inside the sandwich? She hasn't thought of that, has she?

The only things I'm allowed to cut in our house are craft paper and play-dough. With the red scissors.

I did cut Gabby's hair once when I was round her house, but she made me do it. It was definitely her idea, not mine.

The **trouble with Gabby's hair** is it fidgets a lot, so even if you're a really good hairdresser, it comes out wrong.

Gabby quite liked it from the front, but her mum only saw it from the back.

Playing hairdressers is banned in Gabby's house now. So are any games with scissors.

The **trouble with playing round Gabby's house** is she knows all the best places to hide. Whenever she

says, "COMING, READY OR NOT!"
I'm never ready because I'm still
looking for a good place to hide. I used
to hide under her bed but she kept
finding me, and now it's the same
when I hide behind her lounge
curtains.

Trouble is, whenever I say,
"COMING READY OR NOT!" I can
never find her anywhere. Not even
when I've counted to a hundred in
tens instead of ones.

Last time we played hide-and-seek at Gabby's house I was looking for her for ages. In the end I had to give up. And guess where she was?

In the laundry basket with all the smelly socks.

I told her that was cheating because I would never hide in a smelly place like that and so it didn't count and she'd have to hide again.

So she did and then I couldn't find her AGAIN! Even her mum couldn't find her.

That's because Gabby wasn't in the house, she was in the shed. Which is cheating too.

The **trouble with people who cheat at hide-and-seek** is they never admit it.

Especially Gabby. Sometimes, if she's been really cheating a lot, I tell her I'm never going to play with her again.

Trouble is, she always shares her sweets with me, and she's always really good fun too. It was Gabby who taught me how to jump up and down on the sofa and shout,

"Howzatcowpat!" at the same time. The first time we did it round her house on her mum's big leather sofa. Now we do it on my sofa too! Only when my mum's not looking though.

Actually. Thinking about it . . . Maybe I should have a little bounce on our sofa right now. Just to see if I really am getting better. I'll do it extra quietly and I'll whisper "Howzatcowpat" instead of shouting it . . . just in case Mum hears!

Why don't you have a go on your sofa too? This is how Gabby and me do it.

Chapter 13

Twenty whopping bounces and ten Howzatcowpats without laughing! That's really good! Gabby can never do more than six Howzatcowpats without laughing.

The **trouble with laughing** is it can make lemonade come out of your nose. Not when you're doing howzatcowpats – when you're in restaurants.

Once, when me and Gabby were at Pizza Heaven with my mum, Gabby stuck two marshmallow flumps in her ears and pulled a really funny face.

Trouble is, I'd only just taken a drink of my lemonade, so when I laughed, my lemonade didn't go down the right hole. It went up all the wrong holes instead. Then my nose started fizzing and my eyes started watering and my mouth started choking.

Well, sort of choking and laughing at the same time, which is a really hard thing to do.

In the end, my mum had to call a waitress to help her pat me on the back. They made me stand up at the table in front of everybody.

The **trouble with someone patting you on the back** is, if they don't do it hard enough, it doesn't do any good at all, and if they do it too hard, it makes you sound like a seal.

No one had ever heard a seal in Pizza Heaven before, so everyone stopped eating their pizzas and looked at me.

Then Gabby got two dough balls and pretended my eyes had popped out and fallen onto the table, which made me laugh even more.

And choke and splutter.

In the end the manageress came out and took me to the toilets and made me drink a load of water out of the tap. Mum had to rub my back for about ten minutes before we could go back to our table.

Flumps are banned when we go to Pizza Heaven now. And dough balls.

We're still allowed lemonade, but

only if we don't blow bubbles with our straws.

Which reminds me, I need to drink some more water. Mum says if I drink lots of water today, it will help flush all the dib-dab germs away.

Back in a minute!

Chapter 14

Have you ever blown bubbles in your lemonade with a straw? It sort of still works with water and it's quite good in milk. But lemonade's the best.

I tried to do it in a really thick milkshake once, but my mum told me to stop being silly.

The **trouble with being silly** is it can give you scabs.

Not silly with straws – silly with skipping ropes.

At school the other day Gabby and I were doing skipping with Liberty Pearce, except we weren't doing the skipping, Liberty was. Gabby and me were doing the rope.

Anyway, Liberty said she was the best skipper in the school and she said she was the fastest. So Gabby and I went faster with the rope because we thought Liberty wanted us to, but when we switched to super-speed, Liberty wasn't ready, so her legs got caught up in the rope and she fell over and scraped her knees. And she made holes in her tights and she got scabs.

Mrs Donovan said that Gabby and I had been very silly with the rope and that Liberty wasn't a kangaroo and couldn't possibly jump that fast or high. We had to write "We will not be silly with skipping ropes" ten times on a piece of paper during morning break the next day.

Another time Gabby and me were silly with the hosepipe in my garden. No one got scabs, but we did get told off by Mrs Pike. It was a really hot day and Mum had got the paddling pool out of the shed for Gabby and me to play in.

The **trouble with paddling pools** is you have to blow them up with a pump.

Trouble was, Mum couldn't find our pump so she had to do it with her mouth.

So while she was huffing and puffing and blowing, Gabby and me said we'd water the garden. Well we never actually said we'd water the garden, we just did it. While Mum wasn't looking.

First of all we watered the flowers because they looked really hot. Then we watered the grass, which was going a bit brown. Then we watered the shed, which was really brown.

Then we watered Tiptoes.

The **trouble with watering Tiptoes** is he's a cat.

Which means he doesn't like it. Which isn't our fault, because when we watered him, he looked like he really wanted to be watered. I mean, he was right in a really hot bit of sun, all stretched out, not moving even a little bit. Me and Gabby thought he was dying of thirst so we thought he really needed some water.

When the water went on him, he wasn't still any more. He jumped up and went higher than a kangaroo, right over the wall and back into Mrs Pike's garden.

Then Mrs Pike poked her head over the wall and looked at me and Gabby with a cross face and said, "WHO DID THAT TO TIPTOES? HE'S SOAKED!"

The **trouble with holding hose-pipes** is people can always tell which one did the squirting.

So I let go.

The **trouble with letting go of hosepipes** is you can't tell which way they are going to squirt. Which isn't your fault.

Mum said it *was* my fault though. When it squirted her, and made her dress all wet, she said playing with the hosepipe was a very silly thing to do. So did Mrs Pike.

I think that's why Tiptoes stays on the wall a lot of the time now.

Anyway, Mum was so wet she nearly didn't keep on blowing, but then she said that at least if Gabby and I were in the paddling pool, she would know where we were and what we were up to.

We weren't allowed to put the water in the paddling pool after that. Only Mum was.

The **trouble with paddling pool water** is it always gets dead bees floating on it.

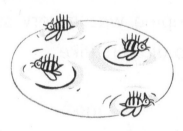

Gabby says dead bees can still sting you, so you have to splash them out.

The **trouble with splashing dead bees out of your paddling pool** is it makes all the water go on the grass.

After three bees we only had a centimetre left.

Mum filled the paddling pool up again for us but said there would be no more after that. She said that water is precious and that if we use too much in our paddling pool, all the oceans will go down, including Mrs Pike's pond, which will be bad news for Freddy.

So the next time we got a bee in our water Gabby tried to splish it out instead of splash it out. Splishes are smaller than splashes.

Trouble is, she splished the dead bee onto her arm. If a dead bee stings you on the arm, your whole body can fall off, so Gabby went a bit loopy.

Luckily it fell off her arm onto the grass. So we managed to trap it under the big red bucket.

Gabby said she was really lucky

to be alive and if her whole body had fallen off, she would never have been able to ride her new bike again. Or do skipping. Mum brought the towels out after that.

Hang on. Where is Mum? I can't hear her in the kitchen and I can't hear her upstairs. Maybe she's in the garden – I'll just go and see.

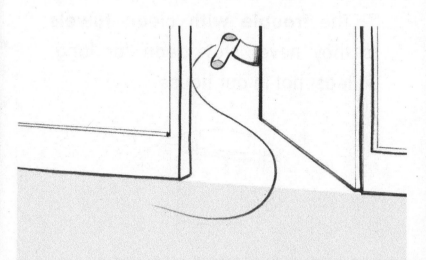

Chapter 15

Thought so. Mum's in the garden, hanging up the washing. She always does the washing on Saturday afternoon. She says if she does the washing on Saturdays, we can start the week with clean towels.

The **trouble with clean towels** is they never stay clean for long. At least not in our house.

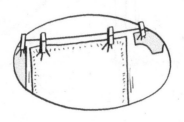

Mum says that the towels would stay clean a lot longer if I got all the dirt off BEFORE I dried myself. She says dirt doesn't wash itself off, it has to be rubbed or scrubbed off. One rub for normal dirt, three rubs for mud, five rubs for grass stains and about two hundred and seventy-three scrubs for snake poo.

I'm not joking. If you get snake poo on you, you are in BIG trouble. Believe me, I know!

The **trouble with snake poo** isn't so much the look of it, it's the STINK of it. It stinks like a hundred stink bombs.

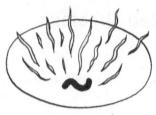

And if it squirts on you, you'll never get it off. And that's just with a little snake, like Dylan Reeves's. Imagine if it was a massive python or something! Imagine the stink then!

Dylan Reeves lives three doors away at Number 38. He's two years older than me, but sometimes he asks me round to play.

It's really good at Dylan's. His mum and dad have got a hot tub in their back garden. And asparagus.

Dylan's bedroom is the best. He's got his own telly in it, and a PlayStation, and he used to have a snake called Shooter.

Shooter was a Colorado garter snake. He wasn't very long – about as long as from my fingers to my elbow – and he was sort of light brown with a stripy crisscrossy pattern.

He lived in Dylan's bedroom, in a tank with a really bright light and heat pads under the sawdust.

Most of the time I just looked at him through the glass, but one day Dylan let me hold him.

I wasn't scared or anything – Dylan thought I would be, but I wasn't. I've always wanted to hold a snake.

But the **trouble with holding snakes** is, without telling you or anything, they can poo on you just like that.

That's what Shooter did to me. I'd only been holding him for about a minute. I was looking at his tongue going in and out when he suddenly started to wriggle.

I tried to stop him from wriggling, but Dylan said I must have squeezed him too hard. Anyway, he pooed all over my hands. That's when I dropped him.

The **trouble with dropping snakes** is they are ten times worse than hosepipes.

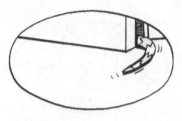

At least hosepipes stay still at one end. Snakes don't. They don't stay still at either end, they just wriggle across the carpet really fast and then disappear out of the door.

That's the last time we saw Shooter. At least that was the last time we saw his face. Dylan saw his tail disappear down a crack between some upstairs floorboards, but by the time his dad pulled the floorboard up with a big hammer, he was gone.

We did find five pence and a paperclip though.

Dylan was really upset. He'd only had Shooter a month. I was even more upset. I had snake poo all over me.

Dylan's dad said it wasn't poo, it was "musk". He said it's the same sort of thing that skunks spray on people when they feel threatened. That made me feel even worse! Now I had skunk poo on me!

I said sorry to Dylan for dropping his snake and went home after that.

My mum said she could smell me when I walked through the kitchen door, and when I made her smell my hand, she nearly fainted.

It took a whole bar of soap, some washing-up liquid, some disinfectant and a dishwasher tablet to get the smell off. Plus I rubbed all the fluff off TWO towels!

Next time I saw Dylan, I asked him if he'd found Shooter. He said he hadn't, but he hadn't given up looking. He said the central heating pipes under the floorboards might act like heat pads and keep him warm so Shooter still might be OK.

Dylan sleeps under his bed in a sleeping bag now. That way he can sleep with his ear pressed to the floor. That way if Shooter wriggles back in the night, Dylan will hear him.

I hope he finds Shooter one day. Stinky or not.

Oh dear.

I just gurgled . . .

Oh dear, I just gurgled again.

Now then . . .

Are those germ gurgles?

Or hungry gurgles?

I'm going to run to the loo just in case. Back in a minute!

Chapter 16

Fantastic news! It was a hungry gurgle! I must really be getting better!

I haven't had breakfast or lunch today, so no wonder I'm getting hungry gurgles.

My mum said drinking water would be all right, but for a while eating food wouldn't be a very good idea at all. She said she got up to rub my back seventy-three times last night and even if I tried to eat anything, it would probably go straight through me.

To be honest, I haven't felt even the slightest bit hungry till now. And even now I don't feel that hungry.

I was opening loo roll number eight this morning when Mum told me I was grounded. She said she didn't like grounding me, but because eating a sweet off the pavement was such a disgusting thing to do, I had to learn my lesson. Otherwise I might do it again. I s'pose she's right.

I promised her I would never ever EVER do it again. And I double promised I would never pick anything up off ANY floor again EVER EVER, except for the toys in my bedroom.

Then I triple promised that even if I saw a hundred strawberry dib-dabs lying on the pavement, still in their packets, with a PLEASE EAT ME sign next to them, I still wouldn't pick them up. Which was a bit of a fib, but I really didn't want her to ground me. And then, for luck, I four times definitely promised I wouldn't even go into a sweet shop again, which is a huge fib, but it was worth a try. I said if I ever saw a sweet shop again, I'd shut my eyes and walk straight past. Cross my heart, hope to die.

But I was still grounded. That's

the **trouble with my mum when she's really cross**. When she says something, she means it.

I suppose at least when Gabby called for me earlier, Mum didn't tell her what I'd done. The **trouble with telling Gabby** is she might tell someone at school.

Like Jack Beechwhistle. If Jack Beechwhistle finds out I've eaten a germy dib-dab, he'll tell my whole class.

And he'll call me names, like Germbelly or Dib-dab Gob. That's the **trouble with Jack Beechwhistle**, he's really good at calling people names.

In fact he's the best in the school.

But I think he's an idiot with knobs on.

So's Fiona Tucker. She sits next to me in class. I used to sit next to Gabby, but Mrs Donovan moved me because Gabby talked too much.

Last month it was "Lend to a Friend Week" at school, so I lent Fiona Tucker my kaleidoscope to play with. And guess what?

She broke it.

She said it wasn't her fault. She said she was walking along the street with her dad, looking at all the different patterns it could make, when she walked into a lamp post.

I was really cross with her when

she told me. I told her she should have been looking where she was going, but she said you can't see lamp posts through a kaleidoscope. You can only see pretty patterns.

I said it was still her fault, because she shouldn't have borrowed my kaleidoscope if she was going to crunch it into a lamp post or anything made of concrete. I was soooooooooo cross with her, I nearly asked Jack Beechwhistle to think up some really horrible names to call her.

Except she got a black eye. It was red to start with, then it went blue, then it went black.

So I didn't think it would be very kind to call her names on top.

That's the **trouble with black eyes**: they make you feel sorry for people. Even if they've broken your toys.

Not if they're boxers on the telly though.

If you're a boxer on the telly, then it serves you right if you get a black eye, because you shouldn't be fighting someone in the first place. And you definitely shouldn't be doing hard punches.

That's the **trouble with boxers**. Black eyes are definitely their own fault.

Unless, I suppose, you're a boxer who's walked into a lamp post, with a kaleidoscope.

Anyway, Mum said Fiona Tucker was a very lucky girl, because if she'd taken my kaleidoscope to the seaside, she might have walked off a cliff with it and fallen miles down into the sea or onto the rocks.

Then she'd have had a lot more than a black eye. She'd have had two black eyes at least.

And anyway, Fiona's dad said he'd buy me a new one. But he hasn't yet.

But he said he would.

. . .

Sometimes, like for instance when I've been told off, I wish I had a dad.

Trouble is, I haven't.

. . .

My dad is dead.

. . .

Because he died.
When I was little.

The **trouble with not having a dad because he died when you were little** is sometimes I wonder what he was like.

Mum says my dad was the best dad in the world, but he would still have told me off if I'd been naughty.

I suppose he definitely would have told me off if I'd eaten a germy dib-dab.

But I can't remember.

That's the **trouble with not**

being little any more. You can't remember.

. . .

However hard you try, you just can't remember.

. . .

. . .

. . .

. . .

And your clothes stop fitting.

Apart from your socks, 'cos socks are stretchy.

The **trouble with growing** is your favourite clothes don't grow with you.

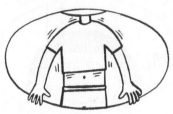

A year ago, my favourite yellow T-shirt used to come down right over my belly button, but it doesn't any more. Neither does my disco top with the stars on.

Mum says I'll be borrowing her clothes soon!

Another **trouble with growing** is the saddle on your bike won't go up any higher either. Gabby got a new bike for her last birthday so her legs look normal when she rides.

My legs look silly on my bike because my knees go too high when I turn the pedals. So I don't ride my bike much any more.

My mum got some spanners out of the garage last week and tried to make my saddle go right up as high as it would go, but when she pulled the saddle up, it came right off the bike! Then it took us ages to get it back on. So now I just leave my bike in the garage.

Mum says if I'm good, I can have a new second-hand bike for my next birthday.

Trouble is, my birthday isn't for three whole months.

Last year I got a remote control car for my birthday. It was white.

To start off with.

The **trouble with remote control cars** is they don't do as they are told.

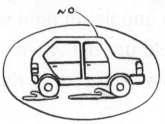

If you try and make them go one way, they go the other, plus if you drive them through muddy puddles, they conk out.

Mum says I shouldn't have driven my car through a puddle. She says it makes the battery wet. That's the **trouble with batteries**. They don't like getting wet.

When I brought my car indoors, she said, "OH DAISY, WHAT HAVE YOU DONE? YOU'VE ONLY HAD IT TWO

MINUTES! IT'S A CAR, DAISY, NOT A HOVERCRAFT. WHAT WERE YOU THINKING OF?"

I said submarines.

Mum said, "GO AND FETCH THE PAPER TOWELS."

After we dried the battery, it still didn't work, so Mum said she would take it back to the shop and complain.

So she did. But that didn't work either because the man behind the counter didn't believe what Mum said.

"PUDDLES! WHAT PUDDLES?" said my mum. "This car hasn't been anywhere near a puddle! IT HASN'T

EVEN BEEN OUT OF DOORS!"

The man said we must have a very swampy carpet because when he opened the boot and shook it, dirty water came out all over his jumper.

I don't do remote control driving any more. I just do parking. Which isn't anywhere near as much fun.

Luckily, Gabby says I can have lots of fun on her new bike, as long as I promise not to fall off and bend the wheels. Or drink all the drink in her drinks bottle. Trouble is, she puts orange squash in her drinks bottle, which is one of my favourite drinks in the whole wide world.

Hold on, I can smell sausages
. . . sausages are my favourite meat
in the world!
Back in a minute . . .

Chapter 17

I was right! It's sausages for tea. With mashed potato, gravy and corn on the cob! If I'm well enough, Mum says I can have some when they're ready, but only if I'm feeling totally better.

Actually I really do feel much better! And hungrier! No gurgles, or anything. I really really think the dib-dab germs might have gone away.

Mmmmmmm . . . there's only one way to be really really sure though . . .

I'll do a hundred Howzatcowpats on the sofa . . .

Start counting . . . Now! . . . I'll let you know how I get on.

Chapter 18

200 bounces! 101 Howzatcowpats!!

And I didn't even want to run to the loo once!

No gurgles either!

I'm better! I must be better!

I wish Gabby would come and call for me now.

Trouble is, I'm still grounded.

Even though I'm back to normal, I've still got nothing to do. I've still got no one to play with, and nowhere to go.

Being grounded is even worse when there's nothing wrong with you.

I wish I could magic myself to a faraway place, where there's loads of things to do. A place like you see on the telly or in holiday magazines . . .

Like Cornwall!

Trouble is, I don't know any words that rhyme with Cornwall either. So I can't do the magic spell.

Me and Mum went to Cornwall for our holiday last year. We stayed in a place called Mevawishywashy, or something like that, and it was so far away, by the time we got there it was dark!

Mum says that's because we should have left earlier. She said when you drive somewhere as far away as Cornwall, you need to get up really early to avoid all the traffic.

Trouble is, I couldn't find my colouring book for the journey, or my other welly. And then when we got on to the big road, we had to go back for my crab line. Otherwise I wouldn't have been able to catch any crabs.

The **trouble with crabs** is they nip.

Especially when you try and get them into your bucket.

One day, me and Mum were sitting on the harbour wall with my crab line when this really big crab grabbed my piece of fish. Mum said to count to ten before I lifted my line, otherwise he might fall off. So I did and he didn't, but when we tried to get him off the fish and into the bucket, his claws bent right back and tried to nip us. And forwards and sideways.

Mum held him over our bucket and tried to shake him off, but he still wouldn't let go. Then he did.

Not over the bucket – right by my leg! So I panicked, and then my welly fell off into the sea, which wasn't my fault, and then the crab fell into the sea too, and my mum kicked over the bucket, and then all our other crabs escaped too and fell back into sea with the big crab!

That's where my mum says they all live now. In my welly.

The **trouble with welly shops in Cornwall** is most of them only sell yellow ones.

Gabby's wellies are green with a frog face, but they didn't have any like those. In the end I got a red pair. They pinch my toes a bit but I didn't tell Mum or I would have had to have yellow again.

The **trouble with yellow wellies** is Paddington Bear wears them.

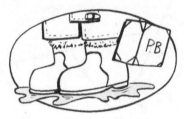

Rebecca Isaacs wore yellow wellies in the playground once and Jack Beechwhistle called her Paddington all day!

That's why my wellies will never be yellow again.

Which reminds me, if Mum un-grounds me tomorrow, I'm definitely going to need my red wellies.

Especially if we make it a really really big mud trap with lots of water and extra mud.

I won't be a moment. I just need to ask Mum where my wellies are . . .

Chapter 19

Mum says my sausages will be ready in five minutes. And she says my wellies are in the shed. Apparently they are still drying out after my last school trip.

The **trouble with school trips** is they should tell you to take a change of clothes. Especially if there are going to be ducks there.

There were loads of ducks at Lime Tree Farm.

The **trouble with the ducks at Lime Tree Farm** is the ones with green heads are far too greedy.

Which means the other ducks hardly get a chance to eat any of the bread that you throw at them.

Gabby and I had saved every last bit of our packed lunch especially for the ducks. Apart from our chocolate biscuit and our tangerines. Gabby said the ones with green heads were daddy ducks. She said if you wanted to feed the mummy ducks and the baby ducks, you had to throw your bread really close to their beaks so the daddy ducks couldn't get to it first.

The **trouble with throwing bread at ducks** is it's really hard to get it in the right place.

Especially if your bread has got strawberry jam on with no pips.

Every time I threw a piece of my sandwiches to a mummy or a baby duck, it went in the wrong place and a daddy duck ate it.

One of the baby ducklings was really cute. He was yellow and fluffy instead of brown and fluffy like all the other ones, and I really wanted him to have a piece of my sandwich without crust on. But even when I pointed to where I was going to throw it, he couldn't get there in time.

If I threw to the left, a daddy duck got it. If I threw to the right, a daddy duck got it. If I did a long throw, a daddy duck got it, and if I just dropped it down the edge, a daddy duck got it.

In the end I got really cross. After about twenty throws, Gabby's sandwiches had completely run out and I only had one piece of my sandwich left.

It was a really nice piece too, with no crust on and oodles of strawberry jam inside.

And I REALLY wanted the yellow fluffy duckling to have it.

And then I fell in. I was kind of hoping it was Jack Beechwhistle's fault, but it wasn't.

I was kind of leaning over the pond trying to get the yellow baby duck to come to me when a load of daddy ducks all came over to me at the same time.

I tried to shoo them away but when I waved them away with my arm, I kind of lost my balance and fell into the pond.

It wasn't very deep, but it was really wet, and the mud at the bottom was really yucky. And my school uniform got soaked.

Gabby screamed, the ducks swam away really fast and Mr Cheetham jumped in to save me.

When everyone realized the water wasn't very deep, they all started laughing. Gabby said they weren't laughing at me, they were laughing at Mr Cheetham. The water only came up to his knees and he could have reached me from the side if he'd wanted.

Mr Cheetham lifted me out of the pond and carried me back to the school bus. Mrs Donovan made me dry myself on a picnic blanket and then I had to empty my wellies onto the grass beside the school bus.

The worst thing was, I wasn't allowed to sit next to Gabby on the way home. Mrs Donovan made me sit at the front of the bus next to the coach driver all the way back to school.

I never did figure out which duck got my last bit of sandwich. I hope it was the baby yellow one. Don't s'pose it was though.

Apart from greedy ducks, Lime Tree Farm is a really good place to go for a school trip. You should ask your teacher to take you. They have loads of animals to look at, including real pigs that are going to turn into actual bacon.

Fiona Tucker says that making

pigs into bacon is cruel, but Gabby said that different animals on farms have different jobs to do. A farm dog's job is to bark at the sheep, a horse's job is to pull wagons, a chicken's job is lay eggs for breakfast, a cow's job is to make milk for cups of tea and a pig's job is to turn into bacon.

We never did work out what a duck's job is though.

I'll go and ask my mum.

Chapter 20

Mum says a duck's job is to stay in the water on a school trip and my job is to stay out of the water on a school trip.

She also says my sausages are ready, so I can have another job.

Washing my hands for dinner.

Sigh.

It's a germ thing.

Sorry about this – I'll see you up at the dining table in a couple of minutes.

That's if you don't mind watching me eat.

167

Chapter 21

Numyumyumyum yum yum nyum
yum yumm yummy yumnum yum
num yum nyum nuyyum yum yum
yummy yum nyum – sorry again . . .

The **trouble with trying to
finish a story with your mouth full**
is nothing you say makes any sense.
All your words are too full of sausage
or sweetcorn, gravy or mash.

Don't worry. I'm going to ask Spiggy, my pet money spider, to tell the rest of the story for me. He's sitting on my shoulder right now.

Say hello, Spiggy.

"Hi!"

Do you mind telling the rest of the story for me, Spig?

"Not at all!"

Otherwise my sausages will get cold.

"Leave it to me!"

Chapter 22

Daisy smiled sweetly at the most handsome money spider in the world (that's me!) and tucked hungrily into her dinner.

Sorry, can you read the words OK when they're this small? OK, I'll shout!

As she raised a fork full of sausage and mash to her lips, her mum leaned across the table and placed a hand on her arm.

"Any more gurgles?" she asked, a little anxious that the dib-dab germs might come back, and more than a little concerned that they only had one loo roll left if they did.

Daisy shook her head, and popped another forkful into her mouth.

"Numyum yum yum yumnuyum yum yum," she smiled.

"Well, I hope you've learned your lesson today, Daisy," said her mum. "You know I really hate grounding you, but sometimes needs must."

Daisy paused in mid-munch. She'd never understood what "needs must" meant but kind of figured it was something that mums just have to do.

"It's OK," said Daisy, "I know picking a germy dib-dab up off the pavement and then eating it was a disgusting thing to do. I have learned my lesson and I don't blame you for grounding me. I'll never do it again. Ever! I promise!!"

Daisy's mum sighed with relief. "That's very good to hear, Daisy. Very good indeed! No one will be happier than me to have a germ-free Daisy back in action again!"

Daisy swallowed a big mouthful of gravy and mash and then raised her eyebrows hopefully.

"So does that mean I'm not grounded any more?" she said, hoping she might be able to start work on the mud trap that evening."

Daisy's mum shook her head. "You're still grounded until the end of the day," she said, "but after today you can play outside again."

Daisy sighed a smallish sigh and then began making plans for Sunday. "So Gabby can come round to play first thing tomorrow?" she asked.

"As long as it's not too first

thing," said Daisy's mum. "I do like to have a lie-in on a Sunday."

Daisy smiled to herself and set about polishing off her plate.

"Mum," she said, gobbling up the last piece of sweetcorn and slurping down the last dribble of orange squash. "Do you know any words that rhyme with 'hippopotamus'?"

Daisy's mum swallowed, frowned and then leaped up from the table and squealed.

"TIPTOESGOTAMOUSE!" she squeaked, pointing in horror at the French windows behind Daisy.

Daisy wheeled round in her chair and stared in the direction of her mum's pointing finger.

There, beside the flowerbed in a pool of evening sunlight, towered Tiptoes. His back was arched, his tail was looped and he was dabbing something wickedly with his paw.

Daisy's mum covered her eyes again as the mouse suddenly twitched, sending Tiptoes into a somersault of excitement.

Daisy sprang up from her chair and raced out of the kitchen door into the back garden.

Grounded or not, if there was a mouse in trouble in her garden, then she was going to be the one to rescue it!

"Scat!" said Daisy. "Shoo, you nasty cat! Leave that mouse alone!"

Tiptoes looked up from the flowerbed in the direction of the kitchen door. His whiskers wilted at the sight of Daisy hurtling across the garden towards him. The very thought of bangs from spade handles and squirts from hosepipes sent him catapulting over the wall.

Daisy's eyes flashed angrily

from the top of Mrs Pike's wall and then anxiously to the flowerbed directly below.

Suddenly her eyes widened and a huge smile crept across her face.

"SHOOTER!!!" she squealed, dropping onto her knees.

It wasn't a mouse that Tiptoes had found basking in the late evening sunshine. It was a snake.

A Colorado garter snake, to be exact!

Daisy snatched Shooter up from the flowerbed, hugged him to her chest and ran back into the kitchen.

"Look, Mum, it's SHOOTER! He's alive!" she shouted, careful not to squeeze too hard. "He's been lost for ages and now I've found him again! Quick, find something for me to put him in before he starts to wriggle!"

Daisy's mum took a nervous step backwards in the direction of the kitchen drawer.

"We must take him back to Dylan right this minute!" beamed Daisy.

Daisy's mum held her best Tupperware bowl out at arm's length and then shuddered as Daisy lowered Shooter carefully inside.

"Dylan is going to be SOOOOOOOOOOO pleased to see him again!" chuckled Daisy, snapping the lid of the Tupperware bowl shut.

"PLEEEEAAAAAASSSSSSSE can we go and take Shooter back to Dylan right now?"

Daisy's mum frowned. She had been awake most of the night and it had been a long and tiring day. Although being grounded had been no fun for Daisy, it had certainly been no fun for Daisy's mum either.

Having a moping, frowning,

grumbling Daisy around the house all day was a bit like living with a small troll.

But rules were rules. Daisy was grounded and that should mean staying indoors, not scampering up the road to Number 38.

Daisy's mum looked at the Tupperware bowl and then deep into Daisy's pleading eyes.

"Very well, Daisy," she sighed, "but you're still grounded the moment you get back from Dylan's."

"It's a deal!" said Daisy, racing to the front door.

"I'll open it!" said her mum,

overtaking her in the hall. "I don't want you squashing yourself against the wall again!"

After a tug and a yank and a heave-ho, the front door sprang open and Daisy raced down the path.

When she returned home ten minutes later, she was a girl transformed. From a small troll to her usual bubbly self.

"Dylan was so pleased to see Shooter again, he nearly kissed me!" she gushed. "Shooter's back in his snake tank now, but Dylan's moved it down beside his bed so he can see him. Dylan sleeps under his bed all the time now. He says sleeping under the bed in a sleeping bag is totally cool. I think Dylan's totally cool too. Trouble is, he's a bit old for me."

Daisy's mum smiled and, with a flap of a tea towel, returned to the kitchen sink.

That's the **trouble with sausage and mash with sweetcorn and gravy.** The washing-up that comes with it.

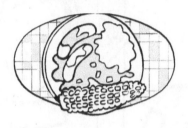

And that's the trouble with this story. There isn't any more to tell.

So that's me done. Glad to be of service. I'm off to spin a web.

Be good, and remember: give spiders a break. You're the ugly-looking ones.

Actually there is a little bit more to the story but it will happen at bedtime, later.

Bedtime, Later

TIPTOESGOTAMOUSE!

That's the word I've been trying to think of all week! Mum said it in the kitchen earlier! Tiptoesgotamouse rhymes with "hippopotamus"! Now Gabby and I can write our magic spell!

I knew if I slept under my bed in a sleeping bag just like Dylan, the magic rhyming word would come into my head!

Mum said sleeping under the bed was silly, and that I should sleep under my covers like normal children. But the **trouble with normal children** is they don't have to write magic spells.

When Mum tucked me in, she made me promise I wouldn't get out of bed. She said, "If I find you asleep under the bed in the morning, Daisy, I'll pour orange squash on your cornflakes."

She was only joking. She wouldn't

dare pour orange squash on my cornflakes. At least I don't think she would.

Anyway, I'm bound to wake up before her tomorrow. She says she's so tired after rubbing my back all last night she'll probably sleep for about three hundred years.

She might even be asleep already.

"MUM!!!!! ARE YOU ASLEEP ALREADY YET??????!!!!!!"

Grunt, snuffle, yawwwwwwwnnnn . . .

"NOT ANY MORE I'M NOT, DAISY!"

. . .

"MUMMM!! DO YOU BELIEVE IN MAGIC SPELLS?"

Grunt, snuffle, gasp . . . "DAISY, THE ONLY THING I BELIEVE IN IS AN EARLY NIGHT. NOW STOP TALKING AND GO TO SLEEP!"

. . .

. . .

"MUUUUMMMMMM! I'VE GOT THE RHYMING WORD I NEED FOR MY MAGIC SPELL."

. . .

"DAISY! WILL YOU PLEASE STOP TALKING AND GO TO SLEEP! THERE'S NO SUCH THING AS MAGIC SPELLS!"

. . .

"MUUUMMMMMM!!!! IF YOU'RE FRIGHTENED OF HIPPOPOTAMUSES,

YOU'D BETTER NOT GO INTO THE GARDEN TOMORROW!!!"

. . .

"AND IF YOU'RE FRIGHTENED OF GRUMPY MUMS WHO HAVEN'T HAD ANY SLEEP, DAISY, YOU'D BETTER NOT MAKE ANOTHER SOUND!!"

. . .

"I JUST THOUGHT I SHOULD TELL YOU ABOUT THE HIPPOPOTAMUS, THAT'S ALL."

. . .

"DAISY. WILL YOU PLEASE STOP TALKING AND GO TO SLEEP! THERE'S NO SUCH THING AS MAGIC SPELLS!"

. . .

Sigh. That's the **trouble with eating a germy dib-dab, being grounded, getting a runny tummy,** feeling better and then trying to tell someone who hasn't had enough sleep about a cat called Tiptoes who's going to turn into a magic hippopotamus on the wall in the garden tomorrow . . .

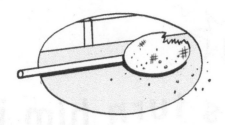

Somehow, they just don't believe you! The end, well, nearly . . .

Tiptoesgota

Tiptoesgota

What a pity,

Let's turn him into

A Hippo

DAISY'S TROUBLE
INDEX

The trouble with . . .